The
GIVING
MANGER

Written by
ALLISON HOTTINGER

Illustrated by
EMILY KING

THE GIVING MANGER

5 little champions, who give
me more than I could ever
give them.

THE GIVING MANGER

ALL YEAR we would wait with joy and delight
To receive a wood toy on Christmas night.
Father would carve them with love and care
Because we had little money to spare.

ONE CHRISTMAS was different. A new tradition began.
On Thanksgiving Day Father told us the plan.
"Children, we will give more gifts this year."
More than one gift, I was thrilled to hear.

"**THE GIVING** will start on the first day of December."
Those days of waiting were the longest I remember.
On December First, I ran downstairs to see
Just what special thing my first present would be.

NO WRAPPING, no ribbon, no presents were there,
Just a simple wood manger Father'd made with care.
"Children, this manger's my gift to you,
Listen, and I'll tell you just what to do."

"THIS CHRISTMAS we'll celebrate the great gift of all —
Jesus Christ born, a baby so small.
Throughout his life, Christ always was giving,
Loving, serving, and never receiving."

"THIS YEAR we will offer gifts back to Him,
By serving others, giving gifts from within.
Each time you serve someone, you also serve Christ —
Remember the scripture we read last night."

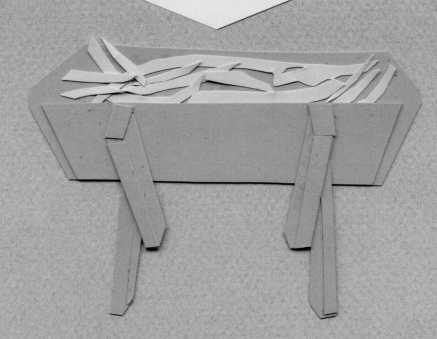

*Inasmuch as ye have done it
unto one of the least
of these my brethren,
ye have done it unto me.*

Matthew 25:40

"AS YOU serve others, you also serve Jesus.
That is the message this scripture teaches.
Each time you serve, put a straw in the manger —
Serve your brother, your mother, a friend, or a stranger."

I FELT sad that this manger was all I would get.
Dad said "more gifts" — I couldn't forget!
I noticed my brother had tears in his eyes.
I could not remember ever seeing him cry.

"I CANNOT believe Dad would do this," he said,
"He promised us gifts, then just gave us this bed.
We don't ask for much, just one measly toy.
Why is he taking our Christmas joy?"

THAT MORNING was filled with frustration and anger.
I wanted to throw away the manger.
But when I got home from school that day,
The manger held ten new pieces of hay.

MY CHORES were all finished, my laundry all done.
A note on my bed said, "Anne, go have fun."
My mother had worked hard serving me.
Gifts aren't always found under a tree.

IT WAS my turn to serve and give to others.
I'd follow the example of Christ and my mother.
I thought about Jesus — that if he'd been there,
He'd want me to love, he'd want me to care.

I STARTED to give by washing dishes,
Then cleaned off Dad's boots and gave him kisses.
I wrote a kind note for my brother Ben,
Placed straw in the manger, went to bed with a grin.

BUT BEN was still mad, refused to join in.
I decided I'd fix it by serving him.
While Ben did his homework, I snuck out the door,
And shoveled the snow, his least favorite chore.

THE NEXT day I saw him put straw in the manger —
Gone was the sadness, disappointment, and anger.
He'd woken up early, heading out to the shed,
Building and painting a baby doll bed.

HE'D MADE this gift for the girl down the street.
They had no toys or money, and little to eat.
I asked my mom if we had food we could spare.
We walked to her house, hoping no one would hear.

WE KNOCKED, left the gifts, and ran away,
Hid behind a bush to hear what they'd say.
Jane opened the door with tears in her eyes —
"Our prayers were answered, look at this surprise."

AS WE walked away, I looked up at Ben.
"We served Jesus, Anne, by helping them.
Now I see what serving really can do:
It brings joy to those you serve, and changes you."

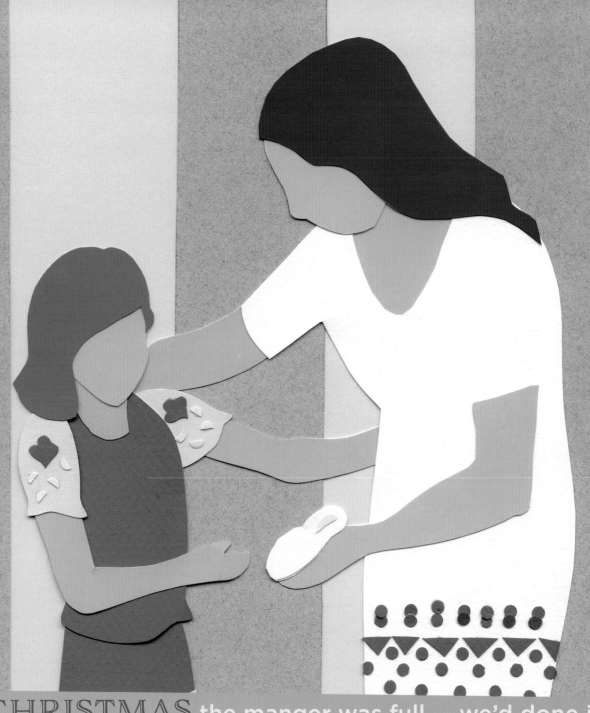

ON CHRISTMAS the manger was full — we'd done it!
Then Father told us there was one more present:
A small baby Jesus, carved by our mother.
So simple, so humble, and like no other.

"**YOU DID** it my children, the manger is full.
Full of service and love, the baby it now holds.
Baby Jesus had no crib for a bed,
But you gave him this manger filled with love instead."

MANGER MEMORIES

Our service through the years

/ / _____
_____
_____
_____
_____

/ / _____
_____
_____
_____

/ / _____
_____
_____
_____

/ / _____
_____
_____
_____

/ / _____
_____
_____
_____

/ / _____
_____
_____

MANGER MOMENTS
Service Ideas

FOR CHILDREN ▪ Leave a letter in a library book ▪ Bake dessert for a neighbor ▪ Pick up litter at the beach/park ▪ Set the table for dinner ▪ Clean up your room without being asked ▪ Compliment a friend ▪ Write thank you notes for your mail carrier ▪ Donate outgrown clothes ▪ Bury treasure at the playground ▪ Make someone else's bed ▪ Pass out stickers to kids waiting in line ▪ Help make dinner ▪ Talk to someone new at school ▪ Wash someone's car ▪ Sweep leaves or shovel snow for a neighbor ▪ Hug someone who is sad ▪ Bring flowers for your teacher ▪ Wash the windows ▪ Donate a book to a doctor's office waiting room ▪ Empty the dishwasher ▪ Take treats to the fire station ▪ Tell someone thank you ▪ Hold the door open for someone ▪ Play with your siblings ▪ Share your favorite toy with a friend ▪ Pass out candy canes

FOR TEENS ▪ Walk dogs at the animal shelter ▪ Babysit for free ▪ Check in on an elderly neighbor ▪ Wrap presents for someone ▪ Wave at kids on school buses ▪ Plan and prepare a meal for your family ▪ Tape change to a parking meter ▪ Clean up a sibling's room ▪ Comfort a friend going though a hard time ▪ Organize or clean out the junk drawer ▪ Bring your neighbors' garbage cans up for them ▪ Collect toys to donate to a local shelter ▪ Take care of someone's pet ▪ Forgive someone who has offended you ▪ Leave kindness stones at the park ▪ Clean the house without being asked ▪ Candy bomb cars in a parking lot ▪ Smile at people in the hall at school ▪ Tell the principal how great your teacher is ▪ Spend time playing with a younger sibling or friend ▪ Write a card to a friend or relative who lives far away ▪ Tutor someone who is struggling in your class ▪ Help someone load groceries at the store ▪ Give someone a ride home from school ▪ Vacuum out your parents' cars ▪ Help someone with homework

FOR FAMILIES ▪ Donate food to the food pantry ▪ Offer an apology you owe ▪ Stuff socks with supplies and give to homeless ▪ Give spare change to the food pantry ▪ Send dessert to another family at a restaurant ▪ Go caroling around your neighborhood ▪ Pay for the person behind you in a drive-thru line ▪ Volunteer at a soup kitchen ▪ Write a note for someone's lunch ▪ Donate used clothes to a shelter or thrift store ▪ Make baby baskets for the NICU ▪ Say hello to everyone you see ▪ Bring lunch to a new mom ▪ Pray for someone in need ▪ Tell someone how much you love him or her ▪ Donate blood ▪ Read a book to your children ▪ Let someone go in front of you in line ▪ Make a meal for someone who is sick ▪ Offer to take a picture for tourists ▪ Collect books to donate to a local shelter ▪ Forgive yourself for any mistakes you've made ▪ Pick up litter at the park ▪ Call a friend you haven't talked to in a while ▪ Say thank you to the bagger at the grocery store ▪ Bring hot chocolate to the homeless shelter

THE GIVING MANGER